The Son of
HUGO GREY

PAULA VAN KERKEN

First published by Paula van Kerken, 2023

Editor: Jennifer Mathews
(www.ballpointpencil.com)

Cover Design and Interior Formatting by Gregg Davies Media (Pty) Ltd
(www.greggdavies.com)

ISBN: 978-0-6397-5715-5 (Paperback)
ISBN: 978-0-6397-5716-2 (eBook)

Additional copies of this book can be purchased from all leading book retailers worldwide.

To my mother.
For all your support and continued belief in me.
You are truly invaluable.

ONE

The worst way to start a Monday was to be stuck in traffic. Unmoving cars queueing up the road, with no end in sight. Dainen Romes sighed and lay his head back in the driver's seat. If things kept moving at this pace, he'd be late for work, and his cranky boss, Wallace, would have a fit if he missed so much as five minutes.

A guy behind him hooted repeatedly and barked an insult, but it didn't look like it would clear up soon. Thankfully for both of them, the cars began moving, and Dainen arrived at Harley's Restaurant only three minutes late. Luckily, his boss's car wasn't in sight, which meant he was late too.

As he walked toward the entrance, Dainen's attention was drawn to an old man walking along the pavement outside the parking lot. He guessed him to be somewhere in his eighties. His green jumper and quaint brown beanie looked like he'd knitted them himself. Dainen smiled. He adored older people. Something about their wisdom and peaceful nature reminded him of his grandparents.

He was about to enter the restaurant when the old man gasped and slowly hunched over, clutching his chest. Dainen's eyes widened as the man collapsed onto the bricks. He instantly dropped his bag and sprinted across the parking lot to the pavement, where he fell onto his knees beside the old man. He wasn't moving.

"Sir," he said quickly, shaking the man's shoulder.

Confused people gathered around to investigate. Whispers surrounded them.

"Please wake up," Dainen pleaded as he checked his neck for a pulse. He was still alive.

He ripped out his phone to call for an ambulance. When it arrived, Dainen got in to accompany the old man to the hospital. As they moved, with the sound of the siren filling the air, Dainen watched him closely. His breathing was slow, but at least he was still breathing. Dainen rubbed his face and let out a little groan. He didn't know this man at all, but he didn't think he could stand it if he died. Not when he'd gotten himself involved and seen his face.

At the hospital, the old man was rushed away while a doctor showed Dainen to the waiting room. He sat anxiously with his elbows on his knees, his foot impatiently tapping on the ground as he bit softly on his bottom lip. How would he explain all this to his boss?

After what seemed like forever, a doctor came walking

toward him. Dainen stood before she'd even reached him. "Is he all right? What's wrong with him?"

The doctor gave him a sad smile. "He had a heart attack," she said, keeping her voice hushed. "Given his age, it's no surprise. He's awake, but his heart is weak. I don't expect he has long. He wants to see you."

Dainen's own heart slowly sank. He gulped and followed her through several hallways to one of the rooms. They entered quietly. The walls were decorated with abstract paintings in soft blues and greens, echoed by the blue-green curtains. The room felt cosy.

The old man's eyes slid over Dainen's face, watching him sit down on the chair beside the bed. "Are you the one who brought me here?" he rasped.

Dainen nodded, swallowing down the lump in his throat. The doctor left, silently closing the door.

"Listen to me, son," the man whispered, "I need to ask you a favour."

Dainen hesitated before asking, "What do you need?"

"Come closer."

Dainen leaned forward. The man grabbed his hand tightly, almost giving him a start, and his dark brown eyes locked onto his.

"What's your name, young man?"

"Dainen, Sir."

"Dainen," he said thoughtfully with a smile. "It means kind-hearted, did you know that? I know we do not know each other, but you look like a good lad, and ... I can't leave without …." He trailed off, his mind seeming to wander as sorrow flickered in his eyes.

Dainen moved him along, gently asking, "What do you need me to do?"

He reached for a folded paper on the bedside table and slipped it into Dainen's free hand.

"My son," he said. "He needs someone to take care of him after I'm gone."

"Your son, Sir?"

"Please."

Dainen cautiously asked, "You mean me?"

"I have no one else to ask, no one who would be willing, anyway. My son is not easy to get along with, but he's everything to me. I just need to know he'll be in kind hands."

Dainen thought it through a long while but finally agreed. "All right, Sir."

"Promise me," he said as he pulled Dainen in closer. "Promise me you'll take care of him."

Dainen held his hand firmly and said, "I promise."

The man closed his eyes, lying back with a weak smile forming on his lips. "Thank you," he whispered.

"May I ask your name, Sir?"

"Hugo," he answered. "Hugo Grey."

A few minutes dragged on until the line on the monitor straightened, a continuous beep filling the room. Hugo's hand went limp.

Assuming he was family, the hospital staff gave Dainen the old man's personal effects, keys, wallet, and the quaint brown beanie. Dainen felt empty when he left the hospital. As he walked down the pavement, a few tears slid down his cheeks, which he quickly dried with a sleeve. He sat on a park bench for half an hour, staring at the distance, before finally deciding to unfold the paper he'd been given. The only contents it held were Hugo's name and address – 77 Gold River Street – not far from the restaurant. That Hugo had been carrying this paper around with him suggested he'd known his end had been near.

Hugo's house could only be described as a mansion. Clearly, he hadn't had any financial issues to speak of. Dainen unlocked the front door and found an old-fashioned interior. Thick carpets, old figurines, and many pictures on the walls. 80s sofas, some candles here and there, probably just for show, and other strange decorations.

He wondered about this son. Considering Hugo's age, Dainen guessed the son would be at least in his thirties. He must have a medical condition that required him to be taken care of, or maybe he had financial problems, which would be strange considering his father's house. Or perhaps Hugo had simply wanted Dainen to offer his son comfort for his loss, but then why would his son be living at home? Would he not live alone by now?

Footsteps emerged from the top floor, approaching the

stairs. As Dainen waited, he anxiously considered the best way to break the news. Then the son appeared, calmly descending the stairs, one hand on the railing, with upright posture and smooth movement. He was most definitely not what Dainen had pictured. His fine blond hair was in a child-like bob shape, and his eyes were bluer than the deepest ocean, almost too blue to be realistic. Definitely contact lenses. His skin was flawless. The three freckles on his cheek were almost mathematically placed. He wore a long-sleeve shirt with blue and yellow stripes and plain jeans, but no shoes, only socks. The strangest part was his age. He seemed no older than seventeen but somehow looked like he had no age at all. He stood at the bottom of the stairs, blinked at Dainen without expression, and gave him one simple nod.

"Good afternoon," he said, not asking any questions about why a stranger was standing in his home.

"Are you Hugo Grey's son?" Dainen asked carefully.

"Son?" he replied. "Not at all. Hugo created me."

Dainen narrowed his eyes. "What do you mean?"

"I am an artificial human created by Hugo Grey."

Dainen stared at him. "Artificial human," he muttered. "What does that—"

"I see I need to put it into simpler terms. I can otherwise be called an android. Or, more casually, a robot."

For a moment, Dainen was unable to reply. When he did, the words came out almost distorted. "Um … sorry, I … don't get it. You're a robot?"

"Casually put, yes. I am not Hugo's only creation,

simply the most successful and his biggest project so far." He tilted his head just slightly. "Who are you?"

"I'm Dainen," he faltered, still having trouble taking this all in. He'd vaguely heard of human-like robots before but never anticipated he would ever see one! He drew a hand nervously through his hair. "Do you have a name?"

"I am called Essai," he replied.

Unbelievable. Dainen supposed it wasn't entirely impossible, but still. Extraordinary.

"So … you're not Hugo's son, then?"

"Hugo has no children or spouse." Essai was idly fidgeting with an ornament he'd gotten from a display shelf against the wall. "However, he does tend to view me as a son figure." He looked up and straightened, saying as a by-the-way comment, "Where is Hugo?"

Dainen winced. Robot or not, he had to drop the bombshell. He made sure to keep his voice gentle. "I'm sorry you have to find out like this, but Hugo passed away today. He had a heart attack. He was taken to the hospital, but he didn't make it. I'm sorry."

The android had no reaction to the news other than an "I see."

"You're not upset?"

"I am unable to experience emotion." He tilted his head in that robotic way again. "Why are you here?"

"Hugo asked me to take care of his son. I didn't think this was quite what he meant."

Essai nodded. "I welcome you."

His blank, neutral face and indifferent attitude made Dainen uneasy. What had he gotten himself into?

Only a few other people attended Hugo's funeral: a young florist in a black dress with a pink bow, two of his old work colleagues, and his neighbour and her husband.

As the pastor spoke, Dainen closely watched Essai, who was blankly staring at the coffin. It was like looking at a living doll. Despite it being a funeral, he wore a red and blue striped long-sleeve shirt. He'd insisted that it was more comfortable and didn't seem to care about, if he even noticed, the strange looks he got from those present.

Dainen pulled his attention away from the robot to observe the coffin being lowered into the ground. Sobbing and weeping filled his surroundings. Dainen shed a few quiet tears himself, and he hadn't even known Hugo. And yet he had entrusted this robot to him. He now understood why the others didn't get along well with his son. How did one 'get along' with a robot?

The florist came over and gently placed her hands on Essai's shoulders. "You all right, dear?" she asked softly.

"I feel entirely healthy," was Essai's detached reply.

The woman gave him an uncertain look and carefully let go of him before turning and walking away, sniffing softly. She didn't look at him again.

After the funeral, they returned to Hugo's home.

Dainen didn't know why, but he somehow felt as if he was intruding. Hugo's lawyer had informed them that the reading of the will would be the following day. There wasn't much to sort out because, apparently, Hugo had left every-thing he'd owned – absolutely everything – to Essai. So this robot had meant more to him than Dainen first thought. Had Hugo been that lonely? Loving an unemotional robot like a son? He guessed one could feel endless love for just about anything if it was important enough to you.

Dainen had collected some of his belongings from his home and began unpacking in one of the spare rooms. His house was far too small for two people to live in, and Essai said he could stay. It was Essai's house now, after all. He looked to the door when a sound drifted from down-stairs. It was music. Curiously, he left the room and slowly made his way halfway down the stairs, stopping when he saw Essai sitting on a couch playing a pan flute. The tune flowed through the house in a serene, soothing pattern. Dainen found himself unable to look away as he descended another few stairs.

When Essai heard him, he stopped playing and calmly looked over his shoulder.

Dainen pointed to the instrument. "I didn't know you played."

"Hugo gave it to me. I've owned it for four years."

"Interesting," he pondered. He cleared his throat. "I'm going to make some dinner. Do you eat?"

"I do not ingest food. I run purely on power supply,

software programs, and hardware." He began blowing into the pan flute again.

Essai hadn't once mentioned Hugo's passing, as if it simply wasn't worth discussing. It disturbed Dainen to think that Hugo had cared so much about someone who wouldn't even acknowledge his death. What was he supposed to do? He doubted he could take care of a human son, never mind an artificial one.

But he'd made a promise. What kind of person would he be if he didn't see it through?

TWO

Dainen's boss started yelling at him before he'd even made it through the door. He made sure to leave the word 'robot' out of his excuse for missing a few days of work, but explained most of everything else. But his boss wasn't really listening, he simply replied with a distant "Hm," gave him a curt warning, and told him to get his hind to work.

Dainen was more worried about whether Essai would be fine at home alone. He supposed he didn't need to be concerned since it wasn't like Essai needed food or drink, and he'd agreed to stay indoors while he was away. He'd been reading a book when Dainen had left, and he seemed to have enough to occupy himself with.

Dainen was rushing up and down to take orders and deliver them. The restaurant was, as always, chaotic and full of noisy people. Waiting tables wasn't his preferred job, of course, but he made good money which was all that mattered for now. If he could save up enough, he could eventually go and study. He'd always wanted to travel the world, so Dainen had his eyes on the tourism industry. But his dream wasn't exactly in sight right now.

A couple raised their hands to call him over. Dainen put on a smile, but the instant he arrived within a metre of the table, the man began snapping, "This meat's rubbish!"

"What's wrong with it, Sir?" Dainen asked, keeping his voice friendly.

"It's undercooked! And we didn't ask for spicy sauce," he complained. "And this? I don't even know what this is."

"All right, I'll take it back and ask for—" Dainen began, only to be cut off by further ranting.

"And my wife's coffee seems to have been warmed in the microwave. Restaurants shouldn't even have microwaves. I expect good service and quality food when I come to a restaurant. I can buy better meat at a low-cost supermarket." The man finally went quiet.

"I didn't cook the food, Sir," he replied patiently.

The man sat back with his arms crossed, let out a sharp "Pfft," and shook his head. "Just take it back and get the right stuff."

Dainen nodded, hiding his frustration, and put the plate onto his tray. As he went to the kitchen, he let out a sigh he hoped no one heard. When he returned with a replacement plate of food, the man thanked him gruffly. He was getting no tip from these two.

He was relieved when the work day finally ended. The first thing he wanted to do when he got home was take a cold shower. So he stripped himself of his uncomfortable clothes the minute he entered his room.

Showered and refreshed, he went down to the living room. The house was quiet. Where was Essai? Dainen called his name, but no answer came. He began climbing the stairs. For some reason, he started panicking inside as he called again.

When a toneless "I am here" came down the hallway, Dainen nearly jumped. He followed the voice to Essai's room and froze at the sight of the cables. The expressionless boy sat cross-legged on his bed, staring at nothing. Two cables stretched from a large machine next to the bed and connected to the nape of Essai's neck.

Dainen gasped as he entered and said quickly, "Are you all right!? What is that?"

"Do not be alarmed," Essai said. "I am simply recharging my energy."

It took Dainen a moment to silence the alarms going off in his mind.

"My energy is currently at seventy percent," he said. "It is wise to keep it above fifty percent. Did you need me for something?"

Dainen stared in shock for a while, then shook his head slowly. "No, it's fine. You carry on." He'd never get that picture out of his head.

After charging, Essai returned to the living room, sat

on the same couch as before, and began reading a history book. Dainen hesitated before approaching him.

"Say, Essai, could I talk to you for a bit?"

He closed the book and looked up, waiting.

Dainen sat on the couch across from him. "I've been meaning to discuss Hugo with you."

Essai blankly waited for him to continue.

"Now that he is … you know, gone … how do you feel?"

Essai tilted his head. "Feel? Please clarify."

"Don't you miss him?"

Essai looked confused.

"How long have you known him?" he tried.

"I was created six years, four months, and sixteen days ago."

"Did you have any hobbies together?"

"Hugo enjoyed reading to me."

"Oh," Dainen said curiously. "What sort of books did he read to you?"

"Examples are *Romeo and Juliet* and the *Sherlock Holmes* series."

Dainen asked him about *Romeo and Juliet* since it was a story filled with emotion and passion, but Essai only explained the plot. The detail was remarkable, Dainen had to admit. He quoted in a toneless voice, "Romeo, Romeo, wherefore art thou, Romeo? Deny thy father and deny thy name——"

Dainen held up a hand to stop him. "All right, I get it.

You have an impressive memory. Did you enjoy reading with Hugo?"

Essai considered the question. "He once read me a story called *Peter Pan*. It was intriguing but entirely unrealistic."

"Was there anything you liked about the story?"

Essai thought about it. "I did not favour any particular character or event."

Dainen tried not to sigh. "I see. Thank you. You can get back to your history now," he said, getting to his feet.

His questions were getting him nowhere. He needed more information about this robot, and more specifically about Hugo. For the first time, Dainen went exploring the mansion. The place was spectacular. It even had a library and four studies. Clearly, Hugo had been quite obsessed with studying. Hugo's workspace was a large room with technology and mechanisms that Dainen had never seen before. He decided not to stay long or tamper with anything he didn't understand. Instead, he left to investigate one of the studies, the one upstairs near Hugo's room. It seemed to be the one in which he'd mostly worked.

There was a bookcase on the left, a blue couch by the window, and an enormous desk against the right wall. His eye caught an interesting-looking hardcover book resting on some scattered papers. He slowly opened the cover to reveal messy writing.

The words on the first page read:

'This journal is all I have to keep me company. Perhaps I can get some enjoyment from it.'

Reading through someone else's journal was hardly proper, but Dainen needed something to go on. Advice, background – anything. So he sat down on the blue couch and began reading. It took him a while to get used to Hugo's untidy scribbling.

'Money cannot buy happiness. I have all the money I could ever wish for, yet I am not as happy as I'd like to be. I have all the equipment and technology I need for my pleasure and curiosity, but I have grown bored. I have no family left in my life and no visitors either, apart from Senna, my neighbour, on some occasions.'

The following entry read:

'Some weeks ago, I created an interesting machine. It can do work, wash the car, clean windows, sweep the floor. It was a cute little robot, but I have broken it down again. Washing windows and cleaning the car are all that keep me distracted and busy these days. If I take that off my list, what do I have left?'

The sound of a pan flute pulled Dainen from his reading. He stared blankly at the wall, listening to the compelling music, then finally returned to the journal, flipping through the pages for something that caught his eye.

'For once, I am rather excited! This one will be unlike any of my former projects. It will take time and require a lot of dedication and patience, but when it is finished, I won't be so lonely anymore.'

Dainen pressed his lips together in pity as he turned to the next entry. The date was a great many months after the one he'd just read. He only skimmed the next few entries.

'August 21.

I have not written in a long time. All the work and time I put in drains me. But I know it will be worth it.'

'September 13.

I cannot get him to move or speak. He is like a doll, sitting limply without purpose. But I swear I will find a way. If this is my final project, so be it. I will finish.'

'January 21.

I have done it! He is finally finished and can walk and talk like a human boy. Quite a handsome young lad, I must say. Clever, too! It feels good to have someone here to keep me company. I don't know whether to thank myself or a higher power for the help, but this is the greatest gift I have ever received.'

'January 26.

I have decided to call the boy Essai. It means *Gift*.'

'March 4.

I thought Essai should take up a hobby. He is rather fond of the pan flute. Plays it for hours! He started with the most horrific sounds, but he's an incredibly fast learner. I bought him a beautifully curved blue flute from an Italian woman's private instrument shop, and he never puts it down.'

Dainen closed the journal and leaned back against the soft cushions, blinking at the ceiling. Sitting around trying to find answers wouldn't help. He had to do something.

The problem was that Essai lacked human experience, therefore, he would not be able to survive in a human world. From what Dainen could tell, he mostly stayed cooped up in the mansion instead of going out to explore things. He was extremely intelligent, but with limited knowledge of people, he couldn't be very street-wise.

If he understood how the world worked, perhaps one day Essai could take care of himself without being restricted by his unusual situation. Dainen wouldn't be around to look after him forever, and he was pretty sure Essai didn't age, which was already a problem on its own.

That's what Dainen would do. Give Essai experience. As the saying goes, 'Give someone a fish, and he'll have food for a day, but teach him to fish, and he'll have food for a lifetime.'

THREE

"I do not need education," Essai said. "I already possess a large enough amount of knowledge."

"Rather see it as an experience," Dainen urged. "School is the first step in most people's lives. I think it would be a good place to start."

"I am not a human. There is no reason for me to live like one."

"You can't stay in this mansion forever, around only one person. You need to get out into the world."

Dainen sat forward, his elbows on his knees. "Look, Essai … unfortunately, people age. They grow old and die, like Hugo did. I can't be here to look after you forever, and you need to be able to take care of yourself. Knowledge alone won't get you anywhere if you lack experience. You need to meet people, explore, see new things, live, and learn. Do you see?"

Essai considered his words and finally gave a nod. "I see. Then I shall try this new experience."

Dainen held up a hand. "Wait, not so hasty," he said slowly. "I'm telling you what might be good for you, but that doesn't mean you don't have a say in the matter. Before we rush into anything, you need to tell me if you're sure. If you're ready. We can wait a while if you aren't."

"What outcome would waiting produce?"

Dainen hesitated. "I suppose you're right. Okay. I'll assume you're sure about this."

The grounds at Hawkendale High School were extensive, large enough to accommodate five football fields. It did have quite a reputation for sports.

After parking the car, Dainen took a deep breath and turned to Essai in the passenger seat. "You excited?"

"I cannot feel excitement."

"Right." Dainen's shoulders sagged a little. "Hey, this should be fun! You'll make friends, learn new things, and maybe even take up a sport. Or take part in music concerts."

"I do not see the benefit of such events," Essai said, tilting his head.

Dainen struggled not to groan but pulled up his shoulders to appear cheerful. "Well, you never know. I'll pick you up this afternoon at half past two, and then you can tell me all about your day."

"Yes." Essai opened the door and stepped out of the car with his school bag.

"See you this afternoon," Dainen said with a smile.

"Goodbye." Essai closed the door and started toward the building, not sparing a glance at the other students. Dainen worried he'd made a mistake. But it was too late to turn back now.

The restaurant was chaotic, and there were way too few servers for that many customers. Why the boss didn't just hire more staff was beyond him, he could more than afford to do so. Wallace was less than happy when Dainen said he had to leave to pick up his 'nephew', but he let him go.

When he arrived at the school, he sat for a few minutes, watching the students pour out of the building, laughing and chatting. All in direct contrast with Essai, who casually walked alone with an uncaring attitude and doll-like face. After getting into the car and fastening his seatbelt, he said, "Good afternoon." And nothing further.

"So?" Dainen said enthusiastically. "How was the first day?"

"Based on my research, it was exactly as I expected a public school to be. I had to correct my Music teacher on her grammar. Other than that, I've encountered no potential issues."

Not the kind of answer Dainen had hoped for, but Essai would be Essai, he supposed. He started the car and pulled out onto the road.

"That's good. I'm going to drop you off at home, then

I need to get back to work, but I'll be back this evening. Did you get homework?"

"I must complete homework for Mathematics, History and English."

Dainen had asked Essai which subjects he wanted, but he'd said it didn't matter what he took. Dainen finally gave in and chose for him. It hardly seemed fair, but Essai was difficult to debate with. English, Science and Mathematics were mandatory, and after serious thought, Dainen chose the subjects he viewed most important for learning about human life: History, Biology and Life Skills. He'd added Music to the list, for it was the one subject that had the potential to spark some form of passion in Essai, and if so, that passion had to be expanded. Essai was highly musical, but it was hard to tell if there was any feeling in it, any emotion. Dainen wasn't a creative thinker in any form of art, so he wouldn't be able to tell. He found himself wondering about it during the rest of his workday.

When he got home, Essai was reading again. He wore a long-sleeve shirt, as usual, this time with yellow, blue, and red stripes. Just how many of these shirts did he have, and why such a fascination with stripes?

"Finished your homework?" Dainen asked.

"Yes, I have. It took five minutes."

Dainen raised an eyebrow. "For everything?"

"I store information I receive through hearing or seeing, and when I need to use it, I simply run a search.

Once I have it, I process the data into the simplest form and write it down. The process took five minutes."

"Interesting," Dainen muttered. He went over and glanced at the open book. "What are you reading?"

"It is a novella I have to read for school. It is called 'Lord of the Flies' by the author William Golding."

"Ah. Yes, I know it well. How is it?"

"It is about a group of children—"

"I know the story. What I mean is, do you find it interesting?"

Essai tilted his head slightly in that odd way of his. "Some of these children possess no common logic. They fight amongst themselves when their energy could rather be used for more important matters."

"I know, right?" Dainen chuckled. "How far in are you?"

"I have ten pages left."

Dainen blinked in surprise. "When did you start it?"

"Twenty minutes ago."

He was dumbstruck. Finally, he just went with, "Well, enjoy."

Later in the week, Dainen sat with Essai to talk about his first few days of school.

"What do you think of your classmates?" he asked.

"The boy who sits next to me in Spanish class has a

habit of shoving his fingers into his nose and then rubbing his eyes. It is very unhygienic."

Dainen cringed. "That's … disgusting. And your teachers? I know I found my teachers annoying."

"How so?" Essai wanted to know.

Dainen winced at the memory. "They had bad tempers and didn't have a lot of faith in us − to put it plainly. They were impatient and not really good at teaching. How are yours? Kind?"

"They are rational enough."

"Ah. Good then. So, is there anyone you'd want to be friends with?"

Essai pondered the question, then said, "You seem eager for me to find a friend. For what reason?"

Dainen was caught off guard. "Oh … I just thought … I don't know, maybe you wanted to."

"Do you have a friend?"

"A few. Most moved overseas, but we still keep in touch."

"What are the benefits of friends?"

"Well, you meet up with them to have a good time together, and if needed, they're there for you, for support. If they're decent, at least." All Dainen's friends were busy people with high-up careers. Meanwhile, Dainen was still stuck waiting tables.

"I need none of those things," Essai said. "I am entirely functional on my own."

Dainen understood. Sometimes, he preferred to be alone as well. It wouldn't be right for him to force Essai.

The best he could do was let things run their path. Things would surely turn out well in the end.

He smiled at himself without humour. Look at him, trying to decide what was best for a robot. How would he know, anyway? He wasn't Hugo, he didn't know the first thing about IT, AI, or whatever this was. He couldn't even correctly reassemble a phone without assistance. What was he doing? He couldn't do this.

"Is something troubling you?"

Dainen jerked a little, returning to reality. He raised his eyes to meet the impossibly blue irises. "Sorry?"

"Something seems to be bothering you," Essai observed. "Or are you tired or sick? It's hard to tell."

No. Dainen couldn't back out now. He'd made Hugo a promise, and he intended to keep it.

"Nothing's wrong," he said with a half-smile, "just deep in thought. I think I need to get some sleep. You don't need anything, do you?"

Essai shook his head.

"Good night," he said as he walked towards his room.

"Dainen."

He stopped halfway up the stairs and looked over his shoulder.

Essai held up his pan flute. "Sound travels all over this house. Would you prefer if I do not play while you are sleeping? I understand some find it annoying."

Dainen stared at him in bewilderment. Was he trying to be considerate? It was true, he could hear the flute at night. But if he was being honest, it was rather soothing.

"No, it's fine," he said. "I don't mind if you play."

Essai only nodded and promptly began playing. A slow, placid melody drifted through the still night.

———

It was Wednesday. Luckily, Dainen had Wednesdays off. The previous week had dragged on forever. Essai was quiet on the journey back home from school. The only sound was that of the radio. Dainen almost got a start when Essai suddenly spoke.

"Two boys and a girl spoke to me."

"Oh?" Hope shimmered in him. "What about?"

"They addressed me as Freak, Weirdo, and Robot Boy. They seemed amused by my lack of emotion."

Dainen took a moment to process. Then he snapped, "What?"

"They said—"

"I heard you." He hadn't meant to snap, but he couldn't stop himself. "What did you say back?"

"Nothing."

"Nothing?"

"I would have informed them why I cannot feel, but you told me to keep that information hidden, so I said nothing."

"You just sat there while they taunted you?"

"Yes."

He took a breath to calm himself, then lowered his voice. "Are you all right?"

"I am not feeling sick."

"No, I mean, how do you feel?"

"I feel entirely healthy." Essai wasn't bothered at all.

Dainen sighed when he stopped at the red traffic light. This wasn't good. They certainly weren't off to a good start. He should have known kids would pick on Essai for being different. Maybe he'd made a mistake, sending him into school life so hastily.

Essai went up to his room, not disturbed by the unfairness of it all, and a while later, Dainen found him at his desk.

"You haven't finished your homework yet?" Dainen said casually, standing outside the doorway. "You're usually done in a few minutes."

"It isn't homework," he replied. "I am searching for information that I do not already possess. It seems that the subject 'Life Skills' contains a lot of such data."

"That would make sense."

"Here, the textbook speaks of various things about families and parents. Healthy family relationships and such."

Dainen entered the room and leaned against the wall. "Do you have questions?"

"Did your household have a healthy family relationship?"

"Very much so, yes. I'm an only child, so I didn't have siblings to fight with," Dainen grinned, but Essai didn't understand the humour. "My parents are kind. They were once quite snobby, but they've moved on from that. Other than that, they're great."

"Define 'Snobby'."

"My parents loved money and the things they could buy with it."

"They are not like that anymore?"

"No. They once owned a successful company together. Made loads of money. But when I was about twelve, it all fell apart. Their accountant had been stealing the pension fund contributions from the employees for years and framed my parents to make it look like they were the criminals. They were arrested and charged, and the company shut down. They were finally found innocent a year later and released from jail."

Essai listened intently as Dainen continued.

"Since the company was gone, they had to start again from scratch. Of course, they still had some money saved, but they weren't good at holding on to it. Plus, before the disaster, they'd lent a lot of money to one of my aunts, who never paid them back. She ran off with some guy to Australia. To make things worse, I was in a private school, which was expensive, so they moved me to a public school, and I had to adapt. Things were messy."

Essai had no reaction. He only asked, "During the year they spent in prison, where did you stay?"

"With my grandparents," he smiled. He hadn't been this nostalgic in a long time. "I enjoyed it there. I adored them to bits, and they constantly spoiled me." His voice softened. "I was devastated when they passed away."

Something flickered in Essai's eyes. He couldn't tell what, but when he blinked again, it was gone. "Your parents lost their money?"

"Most of it. It ruined my plans for college, as well as my parents' reputation."

Essai seemed to consider something for a moment. Then with an expressionless face, he said, "Hugo had a lot of money. You could use some of it to go study."

Dainen's eyes widened. When he realised Essai was serious, he chuckled nervously. "No, no, I can't do that. But thanks for the offer."

Essai tilted his head like he usually did. "How come?"

"It's not my money."

He remained stoic. "If your parents could, would they not have given you money that isn't yours?"

"Y … Yes, but that's different."

"Untrue," Essai declared. "Hugo's money is now legally mine, and what happens with it is my decision. If I feel it is necessary or appropriate to give some of it to you, I will do so."

Dainen quickly disagreed. "Thank you, but it's really all right. I don't need it."

"You said you did."

"I'll find a way to get it on my own. It's your money."

Essai gazed at Dainen for the longest time. Then he sat back in his chair, staring ahead, and said, "Perhaps, but it is much more than I need. Suppose I am to attend university and pay for all the expenses with said money. After I finish my studying, I will have more than enough left. Should I then travel the world and pay for all expenses, there would still be enough for my basic needs for another seven years." Essai went quiet as if he was formulating his next response.

"However," he began again, "I've no need for university, for I have all the logic and knowledge I could possibly require. I also have no need to travel the world, everything I need is right here. Thus, all that this money is currently used for is your basic needs, such as food, drink, and hygiene products."

Dainen hesitated. "Actually, I use my own money for that."

Essai tilted his head again. "Then I see no valid points to your argument. Considering your income, it will not last long enough to pay for your needs and my current school fees and supplies."

A soft smile crept onto Dainen's face. "You should become a lawyer," he chuckled. "You're impossible to argue with."

Essai shook his head. "An argument can only be won if you have valid and logical points."

"Thank you for the offer, Essai. But I'll have to think about it. Hugo left the money to you, after all. If I use it for anything, it'll be used for your needs."

"If you insist," Essai said and continued to read. "The offer will always stand."

FOUR

Dainen frowned in confusion as he watched Essai approach the car. When he got into the passenger seat, Dainen remained silent, waiting for an explanation. None came, so he asked, "Where's your bag?"

"I will need a new one," Essai said bluntly as he shut the door.

Dainen asked slowly, "Why?"

"I do not have it anymore. It will need to be replaced, as will my books."

Dainen searched his eyes for any clue but found nothing. He grew impatient. "I need you to make sense, Essai. Where's your school bag?"

"It was thrown over a fence. I was unable to retrieve it."

"Excuse me?" His voice was sharper than he'd intended.

"I thought it a foolish decision, but those students do not seem to possess rational thinking."

"That's bull!" Dainen rummaged through his bag for a notebook and pen. "Describe them." He scribbled as Essai gave exact measurements to the decimal places, hair, skin, and eye colours. Then he got out of the car and said, "Come with me."

Essai followed. "Where are we going?"

"Show me where your bag is. I'll get it for you."

"It is on the other side of a fence," Essai repeated. "It's unretrievable."

"I'll climb over. Just show me where it is."

He led him to the back of the school building and pointed toward the fence. On the other side was what looked like a storage area. Dainen was about to head over when he spotted a dark-haired boy dropping down from the top of the fence onto a bench, Essai's bag slung over his shoulder. Once he stepped onto the grass, he scanned the school grounds.

Dainen marched over. "Excuse me," he said curtly, "that belongs to Essai."

The teenage boy gave a crooked smile. "Good timing," he said. "I was about to hand it in at the office." He held it out to Essai, who took it without a word. "Not the first time I've saved bags from behind that fence," he added.

The boy didn't fit any of Essai's descriptions.

"I … thank you," Dainen said sincerely.

"No prob," he answered with a thumbs-up before

leaving.

Dainen sent Essai back to the car and stormed into the building, demanding to see the principal.

"I don't care how you handle it," Dainen said to the woman on the other side of the desk, "but this stops now. It's unfair."

"Yes, of course," the principal said. "The well-being of our students is top priority. Thank you for the very detailed descriptions, we'll handle this."

"You're supposed to monitor the school at all times. Why does something have to happen before you act?"

"I deeply apologise, Sir. It will be addressed."

"Good, because if this continues, I'm taking him out of this school."

"I understand." She leaned forward, resting her elbows on the desk. Her face went from apologetic to concerned. "But if you have a moment, Mr Romes, I would like to speak to you about Essai."

Dainen tensed. "What about him?" he asked slowly.

"He isn't terribly sociable. He seems lonely and isn't making an effort to make friends. He is extremely intelligent, I tell you, we've never seen a student like him. But his behaviour is quite strange. Is he all right? Has he been through any form of trauma? Or is he simply an introvert? I realise this is personal, but maybe we could offer some guidance for him."

Dainen shifted uncomfortably. "Well, he … lost his father."

Her shoulders sagged. "Oh, dear. I am sorry to hear that. Can we be of any help?"

"Thanks, but I'm doing okay with him on my own. Just please sort out the bullies."

Teenagers poured out of the school building, and Essai finally emerged, this time with his school bag. Dainen was a little surprised when a cheerful group stopped Essai on his way to the car, offering him what looked like coffee. The bully issue seemed to have been sorted out quicker than he'd expected.

He watched Essai say something. If Dainen's lip-reading was accurate, it was, "I do not drink." The teens somehow convinced him that he should. Essai was about to take the cup from the girl when she tipped it over his head, and hot coffee poured all over him, making Dainen shudder. The children laughed and gave each other high-fives. Essai's blond hair was tinted brown, and coffee ran down his striped shirt, and all he did was wipe his face and stare at them.

Dainen couldn't control himself. He stormed over, and it took every last bit of his resolve not to thrash these kids. He kept his voice down as much as he could to avoid a scene, but he made sure to get the message across that they were to stay far away from Essai. They mumbled weak apologies, and taking Essai by the elbow, Dainen led him to the car, where he instantly searched for a cloth to dry him.

"Look at me," Dainen murmured, gently lifting his chin to clean his face. Essai didn't shift as he dried his hair, neck, and shoulders. "Does it hurt?"

"I have a chip installed that allows me to experience a version of pain." There was indeed a hint of pain in his even voice. "Hugo wanted me to be able to feel as many human sensations as possible. It feels hot."

When he finished drying him, he threw the cloth on the floor of the car and sighed again. "Essai, are you okay?"

"It doesn't hurt anymore. I feel cold now. And wet."

Dainen sat back and stared at the roof in disbelief.

"Why did they do that?" Essai asked in his usual neutral tone. "It does not seem to benefit them or anyone else."

"They're bullies," he grunted. "It's what they do. Because they can. Because you're an easy target. To make themselves feel superior. Because they get no attention at home. Take your pick."

Essai stared at him blankly before reverting his eyes.

"God," Dainen breathed softly, burying his face in a hand. "I'm so sorry, Essai."

"Why are you apologising?"

"I should've seen this coming. Rushing you into this without any proper thought was inconsiderate of me." He said sincerely, "But I promise this won't go on."

Essai nodded once and said nothing more about the

incident.

"Just … take a shower when you get home. You said you can handle water?"

"The outer layer of my body, the mimic of skin, is waterproof."

Dainen started the car and said, "It'll be all right. Let's get you home."

The sounds of Essai's pan flute flowed gently through the house. Dainen had also showered and was headed downstairs to the kitchen when he froze with a frown upon seeing Essai on the couch. He was wearing a familiar green knitted jersey much too big for him and nothing like what he usually wore.

Dainen raised an eyebrow. "Essai?"

He stopped playing and looked up vacantly.

"Is that your jersey?"

"No, it's Hugo's."

"Why are you wearing it?" he asked cautiously.

"I have simply decided to." He left it at that and continued playing.

Dainen would have understood why if he'd been human. But he wasn't human. He didn't know what to say further, so he left it hanging. The melody stopped as he entered the kitchen, and silence covered the house like a cloak. Then, as if after a waver, the music continued, not a single error in the tune.

FIVE

The classroom was quiet, apart from the ticking clock on the wall. Baldovino lightly tapped his pen on his knee, staring at the last question before him. Man, he hated Maths. Why'd they have to write a class test every Friday?

Find X .... Find X ....

His eyes drifted to Lenne in the row in front of him. She was focused, and her hand was moving almost nonstop, only now and then lifting to tuck a strand of dark brown hair behind her ear. She was wearing a white tank top with baggy trousers. Rather attractive. He'd have to tell her that after this boring test.

His eyes returned to the paper. Find X. Baldovino felt inclined to circle the X and write, 'Here it is.' Ah, what the hell, why not?

When the bell finally rang, he was the first out of the classroom. He waited outside until Lenne emerged and said, "Hey, *Amore*." Being Italian, Baldovino often used such phrases.

She walked over with a quirky smile. "You were suffering there," she teased.

"Yeah, they told me to find X, but I guess it ran off. Did you see it?"

She smirked. "The answer was six."

Baldovino wrapped his arm around her shoulders as they started down the hallway and murmured, "By the way, you look totally hot today."

"I always look hot, *Tesoro*."

That was true. Lenne was the only person he knew who wasn't fake and plastic. And besides that, she was just plain awesome. She always wore her hair down and never wore makeup because she didn't like how it felt on her face. She saw it as hiding one's true self. A few dark freckles on her nose bridge complemented her dark hair and eyes.

Lenne wasn't as outgoing and social as Baldovino. In fact, she was more of an introvert. She preferred one or two good friends rather than a huge group of fake ones. She wasn't the type to pretend or try to please everyone to raise her reputation. That was probably the main thing that had drawn them together – they were the only real people, surrounded by plastic, two-dimensional fakes.

Vino, as most people called him, was more of an extrovert. He liked chatting with crowds of classmates – one of the things that made him popular. He guessed, in a way, he was a little fake too. It hadn't been his choice to be so well-liked, people just found his personality magnetic. He only greeted back and played along because he knew school would be over soon and he planned on never seeing these dorks again. Finally, he and Lenne would be free.

Although Baldovino looked like the typical trendy guy, it wasn't to boost his reputation at all. He wore denim jackets and black T-shirts, not to make people think he was cool, but because he felt comfortable wearing them. He liked his black hair messy but in a stylish way, almost like those Anime guys. It wasn't about what others thought, but how he felt – and it made him feel free.

"Hey, Vino, Lenne," a friendly voice called from a locker. "How you doin' guys?"

He waved. "Cool, Dave. You?"

"Good man, good. D'you do your English homework?"

Vino flinched. "We had homework?"

Lenne smiled, but she didn't like all this attention. Baldovino had been well-liked all his life. He'd warned her about that back when she'd first put out the idea of them dating. But she'd still chosen him and hadn't turned back yet, for which he couldn't be more grateful.

Vino leaned in and was about to whisper something romantic when he was interrupted by the familiar sound of someone crashing against a locker.

"Sounds like trouble," Lenne said, hurrying towards the commotion, Vino falling in step beside her.

Around the corner, they found a blond boy being

repeatedly shoved against a locker by a pack of boys – typical of the football players.

Hey, he knew that boy! It was the guy whose school bag he'd retrieved from the other side of the fence.

"Steve and gang!" Baldovino growled.

Both the boy and the bullies turned their heads to stare at him. The leader was gripping the guy's shirt, but the blond didn't look like he cared.

"He's half your size. What's wrong with you?" Lenne grunted.

Vino stepped forward, hands in his pockets and gave them a crooked smile. "Seriously, guys, this is just sad. Do you really have that little to do with your lives?"

"You stay out of it," their leader, Steve, scowled.

"See, I'm already in it," Vino advanced, "so, what happens now? Do I snitch on you? 'Cause let me tell you, I've got a lot to snitch about." He let out a laugh, and the gang tensed. "Did you know skill-enhancement drugs are forbidden in sports? If you get found out, you'll be kicked off the team. And that sucks 'cause football's the only thing you've got going for you."

Panic flashed in their eyes.

"So why don't you leave this guy alone? How's that?"

They knew well that Baldovino wouldn't hesitate to turn them in, so they were quick to make themselves scarce. He grinned in triumph as Lenne approached the boy.

"You okay?" she probed, placing a hand on Essai's shoulder.

"I am not hurt." He didn't seem bothered at all.

"Remember me?" Vino said. "Guy with your school bag?"

"I do remember," he said in a toneless voice.

He stuck out his hand with a smile. "You're Essai, right? I heard your dad call you that. Name's Baldovino. This here's my girlfriend, Lenne."

Essai shook their hands.

"You can call me Vino. Lenne doesn't like shortened names, but she's fine with L."

"You should be called by your full names," Essai stated. "I shall call you Baldovino and Lenne."

Vino raised an eyebrow. "If you insist. So, where's your friend group?"

"I do not have a friend group," he said. "I am on my own."

"Damn," Vino muttered, "Sorry, man. What about us? We can be your buds."

Essai tilted his head. "Buds?"

"Friends," Lenne clarified. "We see no reason for you to be alone."

Essai nodded. "Very well."

Vino shrugged at Lenne and returned his glance to Essai. "Well, lucky for you, we're popular. Since you're with us now, no one will dare touch you again."

"Disgusting system if you ask me," Lenne grumbled, "but that's how it goes here."

"Welcome aboard," Vino said with a grin.

"How was school?" Dainen asked.

"You might be satisfied to hear that I have acquired two friends."

Dainen's brow shot up. "Honestly?"

"Indeed. Their names are Baldovino and Lenne. They gave me assistance when I needed it."

Some of Dainen's excitement was replaced by concern. "Assistance with what?"

"A group of boys pushed me against a locker door for no clear reason. Lenne and Baldovino made them leave."

"The bullying hasn't been sorted out yet?" Dainen snapped.

"Baldovino says I am untouchable since the two of them are popular."

Popular kids were usually bad news. But Dainen held back those words and sighed. "Good grief. I promise I'll get it all sorted out. So, tell me about these two. What did you say the guy's name was? Bell …."

"Baldovino," Essai corrected.

"Sounds Italian. Interesting. And the other one?"

"Lenne," he answered. "I believe they are romantically involved."

"Hmm. And what are they like?"

"From what I could tell, Lenne is fond of the subject IT, and Baldovino isn't fond of any subject but particularly dislikes Mathematics."

Dainen laughed. "Baldovino sounds like me."

Essai was the strangest guy Vino had ever come across. His face was always expressionless, his hair seemed almost plastic, and his eyes bluer than his mother's bright bedroom curtains. He spoke in a one-tone voice, using perfect grammar, and always wore shirts with stripes. He'd also never seen Essai eat or drink.

At first, he was wary of asking, but his curiosity got the better of him, so Vino asked Essai to explain. He hadn't pegged him as someone who made jokes, but he'd hit him with, "I'm an artificial human." He decided not to ask further.

It was Wednesday, about three weeks since they'd met Essai. Lunch hadn't come soon enough. Vino put his textbooks in his locker and made his way to the dining room, where Essai and Lenne were already seated and talking. After getting his food, Vino walked as quietly as he could to the table so he wouldn't be heard. He came up behind Lenne on tip-toes, leaned in, and whispered beside her ear, "Boo."

She jerked with a sharp gasp, and he chuckled as her head whipped around. She clicked her tongue and gave him a light shove. "Jerk."

But as he sat beside her, he spotted a smile on her lips from the corner of his eye. He grinned and extended a fist over the table. "Hey, Essai."

Essai stared at the fist for a few seconds, then reached over, opening Vino's hand so he could shake it.

"You don't know what a fist bump is?" Baldovino asked with surprise. "You punch it, not shake it. It's a type of greeting."

"It is not a formal greeting," he responded.

"Yeah, it's not supposed to be formal. We'll work on it."

As strange as Essai was, he was good company. His range of knowledge was near impossible. He knew almost everything there was to know about history, mythology, science, religion, philosophy – anything. Lenne spoke to him about IT most of the time, and he knew much more than her, which was mind-blowing, considering Lenne knew almost everything about IT. And when they argued about certain tech issues, it was the weirdest thing, Essai never got upset. He was so calm, yet never backed down. He never seemed to consider he could be wrong. Baldovino wouldn't know which was right anyway, he wasn't a tech guy.

When the bell rang, they got up, and Lenne let out a heavy sigh. "Let's agree to disagree," she said.

"If you prefer," Essai responded blankly.

She rolled her eyes but smiled. "It's a grey area anyway."

At Essai's Music classroom, Vino and Lenne greeted him and continued to their Maths class. For a while, they didn't speak.

Vino finally said, "Hey, Lenne. I've been thinking. Remember when Essai told me he's a robot?"

Lenne scoffed softly. "What, you believe him?"

He narrowed his eyes in thought. "I guess not, but think about it. His grammar's almost flawless, he knows just about everything, and he's just so—"

"Come on, Baldovino, don't be absurd," she chuckled.

He thought for another moment. "With the technology of this age, you don't think it's possible?"

Her eyes turned to him as they entered the classroom, where kids sat on the tables, laughing and chatting.

"I didn't say it's impossible. But highly unlikely," Lenne said as she sat in her seat, and Vino took his in front of her.

He turned in his chair to face her, laying his elbows on the backrest. "But it's possible, right?"

"Yes," she sighed, "maybe."

The teacher walked in, and the kids rushed to their seats, some still giggling.

Lenne whispered, "Essai's strange, yes, but he's not a robot. Things like that just don't happen."

SIX

"So you're saying it's finally dealt with?" Dainen barked down the phone.

"I can't be certain yet, Mr Romes," the principal replied. "All I know is that Baldovino and Lenne reported four boys, and they've been suspended."

"Four boys? No, that can't be right. I saw a girl in the group the other day. They threw coffee over his head. What about them?"

"I'm not sure who you are referring to, Mr Romes, but believe me, we are trying to find as much information as possible. We've called Essai in to describe them for us, but he didn't know their names. Unfortunately, Sir, he described many of our students."

Dainen frowned. "Many? Jesus! How many bullies do you have at your school?" He pinched his nose bridge, trying to calm himself.

"However, Essai says it's stopped."

Dainen remained quiet, staring at the carpet. Finally, he swallowed and said softly, "Thank you. I hope you're right. Just … keep a lookout for me, okay?"

"Of course, Mr Romes."

After the phone call, Dainen needed a distraction. Shopping wasn't a usual way for him to pass the time, but the house needed a few things anyway. He decided to take his time wandering through the aisles, but it wasn't helping much to relieve his stressful thoughts.

This was his fault. Because of his hasty and inconsiderate decision, Essai was suffering, and that's not what he'd intended. A human experience, meeting people, making friends, exploring the outside world – not this. He was supposed to take care of him, dammit! He'd promised to keep him safe, and now? He was failing both Hugo and Essai.

After about an hour, he returned to the car. He sat in the driver's seat for some time, his seatbelt still hanging beside him. Then he took out his phone. He'd given Essai a phone when the bully problem started because he needed someone to call if there were any emergencies. He tapped on Essai's name and held the phone to his ear. It rang twice before it was answered, and he was almost too relieved when he heard Essai's voice.

"Good afternoon."

"Essai, hey," he breathed. "What are you up to?"

"I am currently in the dining hall with Baldovino and Lenne."

"Oh, good. Just thought I'd check on you. Every-thing's okay, right? Nothing bad has happened today?"

"If you are referring to bullies, I have not encountered any."

"Good," he breathed. "Just checking. Call me if some-thing's wrong. I'll see you later."

"Yes."

The call ended, and Dainen sighed in relief. He hoped this meant the end of it. If it went on, Essai would have to change schools. But then he'd lose his only two friends, and there was no guarantee another school wouldn't have the same problems. Perhaps they'd be even worse. At this point, he was stuck between a rock and a hard place.

Private study was the most boring time of the day, to be used strictly for studying or doing homework. For Vino, it meant sitting with open textbooks and staring at the walls. It wasn't like he would use the time for Maths homework. Why would he do that? Unlike Lenne, of course, who was diligently reading.

Vino checked the time. Essai hadn't shown up yet. He leaned across the table and whispered as softly as possible, "*Amore.*"

Her eyes lifted to meet his, and she raised her brow in question.

"Where's Essai?"

Lenne leaned forward too and whispered, "Signed out to use the music room."

"Oh."

Silence covered them again. It didn't look like Lenne had much to do either since she'd already finished her homework during break, so he leaned in again. "*Amore.*"

She gazed at him.

"You want to get out of here?" he winked.

Essai had decided to use his study time to practice music. He'd been told playing his pan flute in the study hall itself would be inappropriate, so the music room was best. But he didn't see the tall boy exiting the room in time, and they walked straight into each other.

Instead of letting it go, the boy snapped, "Watch it, jerk!"

Essai noticed he was twenty-three and a half centimetres taller than him and about five centimetres wider. The boy's hair colour was similar to peanut butter, and his eyes an amber brown. His skin seemed dry and clearly needed care.

Essai went around him, but the boy yanked him back by his elbow.

"Where's my apology!?"

Essai tilted his head. "Walking into you was a mere accident. I see no benefit in an apology."

It was the correct answer, but it did not seem the boy appreciated it.

Before Essai could react, the boy grabbed the collar of his shirt and hissed in his face, "Listen here, you twit. I've had a crappy day. So if you don't apologise to me immediately, I'll bash your damn face in."

"It is unnatural for a person to become aggressive in a situation like this," Essai said. "I have read a few psychology books. Going according to those texts, I would propose you visit an anger management—"

"What the hell did you just say to me?"

Essai did not expect the powerful blow to his face. His head shot back, and he collapsed onto his back, pain surging through his body.

"You just dug your own grave," the boy raged. "Why the hell is everyone on my case today!? Can't I be given a break just once?"

"Talking to me about the subject has no relevance," Essai groaned. "I have a lack of context."

A heavy boot crashed against his side and, not long after, into his shoulder. To Essai's surprise, a cry escaped his mouth.

"I see you around, bragging about your damn knowledge and whatever," the boy continued to shout. "I'm sick of people thinking they're more clever, stronger, better looking, or whatever than me!" He booted him again, and Essai cried out once more, then gasped as pain shot up his side. "See? Who's weak now?"

Essai heaved, finding it a little harder to breathe. "You

broke something," he warned. "I advise you to stop—"

Another kick came, then another. Then the boy grabbed his collar, yanked him up, and Essai was driven back, crashing hard into a wall. He whimpered. He didn't know he could make these sounds – he'd never been in this much pain.

"I'm always getting beaten up, and I'm sick of it! Now it's my turn. Does it feel good? Huh?" The boy sent a knee into his stomach, and Essai jerked as an electric spark travelled through him. That was serious. A few more knees, finally an elbow to his side, and then the boy dumped him on the floor, growling, "Everyone needs to just stay out of my way." And then he left.

Essai twitched, there on the floor, as a shock went through him again. Another, and he let out a little gasp. Pain in his back, pain in his stomach, his side, his shoulder. Another shock, another jerk. Another gasp and his fingers began tingling. He'd never felt this sensation before.

He wanted it to stop. It was uncomfortable. No, more than that – it was painful. And he wanted it to end.

His mind began racing as he ran possible outcomes through his head, the potential problems, and the best solutions. He concluded that he had to call someone to aid him. Dainen had said to call him. But he was far away. By the time he arrived, it might be too late.

Essai's actions were delayed. His arm only moved two seconds after he willed it to. It took him almost two minutes to finally get a hold of his phone and pull it out.

His hand jerked when another shock went through him, almost dropping his phone. He took in broken, unsteady breaths as he went through the names on the screen. Stop. He wanted it to stop. Stop…

There was someone close enough to help him. The highest probability of success. After a pause, he tapped on the name and brought the phone to his ear.

Lenne giggled as she pulled Baldovino into the tiny abandoned classroom. They had also signed out of study time to go to the 'library'. Vino grinned at her, closing the door before taking her by the hips and pulling her against him, making her giggle again.

This classroom had belonged to an English teacher, but after an incident that the faculty refused to talk about, he was fired, and the classroom was emptied. And it had remained empty. It was a waste of a big classroom but a cool place to hang out during free periods.

Lenne grabbed Vino's shoulders and pulled him in to start kissing him. They rarely got a chance to kiss at school. And after school, Lenne was mainly studying, so when an opportunity slipped in, they took it. Lenne slowly moved him back until he was up against the wall, then cupped his face as they kissed. Baldovino's hand travelled to her lower back, then her shoulder, then her hair, then her lower back again. They pulled apart for a second, and Vino grinned at her.

"This place is dusty," he whispered. "Hardly romantic, *Amore*."

"Don't be picky," she teased and kissed him again.

His phone buzzed in his pocket. He ignored it. Finally, he was broken out of his trance when Lenne whispered, "*Tesoro*. Your phone."

"Oh, right." He reached for his pocket as Lenne nuzzled the inside of his shoulder. He frowned at the screen. "It's Essai." She pulled away, and he gave her a wink. "Be right with ya." She grinned as he answered the call. "Essai. What's up?"

There were a few moments of silence, then broken, ragged breathing.

Vino's brow furrowed. "Buddy? You okay?"

Essai finally said, calmly but with pain in his voice, "I'm broken."

Vino swallowed as his body went cold. Lenne looked puzzled, so he put the phone on speaker. "What do you mean, dude? What's wrong?"

Gasps cut off his words. "I … walked into a … a boy. He damaged me. I believe something inside me is … broken. I require assistance."

Vino's eyes widened.

"Where are you?" Lenne asked quickly. "Still in the music room?"

"Yes. H … hurry."

"We're on our way," Baldovino said. He shoved his phone back into his pocket, and they rushed out of the empty classroom.

SEVEN

"Oh man," Vino shuddered, running a hand through his hair as he stared at Essai lying on the floor. He wasn't moving. "Ah hell, this isn't good!"

Lenne instantly crouched beside him and began examining him. She frowned. "No bruises," she murmured, then lifted his eyelids and leaned in to look at his eyes, tilting her head. "Strange. Essai. Hey, can you hear me?" She shook him gently. "Come on, answer me."

Baldovino swallowed nervously. "Do you think he has a concussion?"

"I'm not sure."

She began feeling his sides, probably for broken bones. Would you be able to feel if someone's bones were broken? Vino didn't study Biology. Then again, neither did Lenne.

She gasped after she touched his neck.

"What?" Vino said quickly, coming closer. A weird

line spread across Essai's neck, like a thin indentation. Vino went cold. "What did you do?"

"I was just checking for a pulse!" she defended. "But I didn't find anything." Her voice was trembling, but she soon got it under control and watched as another line formed on Essai's neck. Then one on the left and the right, forming a perfect square.

"The hell's happening?" Baldovino exclaimed.

Lenne said nothing, just pressed her lips together and felt the area, frowned, and said, "Wait … this is …."

She opened it. Opened it like a door. And inside was a port, maybe for a charger of sorts.

"No way," Vino gasped. "Lenne, I told you. See, I told you—"

"That doesn't matter right now," she said impatiently and handed him Essai's phone. "Call that guy he spoke about. Dainen." She continued examining him, looking for more places to open him up as Vino searched through his phone.

"Ugh, this is a disaster," Lenne moaned. "I don't know what's broken and where or how to get to it."

"Maybe we should … I don't know, charge him?"

"Charging him won't help us if he's broken," she sighed.

Vino dialled Dainen and waited. He recognised the man's voice.

"Essai?"

"Uhh, not Essai," he said. "Baldovino here. Hey, uh, there's a bit of a problem."

Panic laced the man's voice. "What happened? Where's Essai?"

"He's with us. He had an encounter with a kid and … Aw man …."

"Just give it here," Lenne said calmly, holding out a hand.

She was always more levelheaded in these situations, so Vino gave her the phone.

"Hello, Sir," she said, "Essai got beat up. He called us to help. He said he's broken somewhere, but I don't know where to look. He feels hot. I think the fan may have been damaged, but I'm not sure how this kind of technology works."

It was amazing how composed she was, Vino thought. Wasn't she panicking? Then again, Lenne was always cool under pressure. Vino bit his lip as he watched her listening to Dainen, her brow furrowing in concentration.

She nodded, "Yes, Sir," and hung up. "He's on his way. We'll have to sneak Essai out somehow. Dragging out a limp guy will bring questions that we won't be able to answer." She took a deep breath, removing a strand of hair from her cheek. "There's a gate nearby and an old shed right next to it. We can take him there."

"Right," Vino swallowed. His heart was pounding out of control, no matter how much he willed it to slow down. Lenne noticed.

"Hey … *Tesoro*." She got up, went over, and gently brushed his cheek. But her eyes were serious. "I need you to be steady, okay? You're going to have to help me here."

He took a deep breath, and calmed himself, then straightened up. "Okay. What do you need me to do?"

"First, help me get Essai to the shed. Then go to the office and sign him out. Say he has an appointment or something, and he sent you to sign him out while he got ready. You'll be fine. You're always making up excuses for being late or not doing homework – you're good at spinning stories." Lenne grinned.

Despite everything, Vino let out a chuckle. "Yeah. Yeah, I can do that."

"Stay calm. Essai will be fine if we get him out of here. Then we can get back to making out. What do you say?"

Baldovino smiled and whispered, "Sounds good. Let's do this."

Lenne kissed him on the cheek, returned to Essai, and took him under his arms. Vino took his legs.

"Be careful with him," she warned. "If something's damaged or broken, we need to be gentle."

***

Dainen sniffed impatiently as he wiped the sweat from his forehead, continued paging through the journal, and now and then searched around the workshop for different parts and mechanisms. Essai lay on a large brown couch against the far wall, not moving or opening his eyes. By the time Dainen had reached the school, Essai was almost too hot to touch. Dainen had positioned three fans to blast over him.

He paged through the book frantically, wiping his face again, just as a tear escaped his eye. He should've seen this coming. He knew Essai was in trouble, so why hadn't he done more? Why hadn't he tried harder? He could've used Hugo's money for a private school – or at least something safer. There were so many things he could've done better. Instead, his actions had led to this.

He took a deep breath and forced down his guilt, forcing himself to focus. Hugo had used this particular journal to note precisely how all Essai's parts and pieces worked, inside and out. On the very first page, he had written:

'To whom it may concern, in case I am no longer around: A detailed and precise guide to Essai's body.'

Within these pages, Hugo had listed and described every possible thing that could go wrong with Essai – how to determine what was wrong and how to fix it. Dainen had all the recourses he needed in the workshop. All he could hope for now was that he had enough time.

"And now," the principal paused, reviewing her notes. The assembly hall was quiet, apart from the faint whispers here and there. "Oh," she said, "it seems that Baldovino Mori and Lenne Anderson have an announcement this morning."

Half the school erupted into cheers, laughing and chanting their names.

Lenne glanced at Vino. "Ready to do this?"

"Ready," he said.

They got up, and everyone applauded as they made their way to the podium. The principal smiled and stepped aside for them to come up to the microphone.

Lenne took a deep breath and spoke first. "Good morning, everyone. As much as you were all cheering just now, I'm afraid this announcement is no laughing matter – it's serious."

Since everyone loved Lenne and Vino, they waited patiently.

"This school always preaches that students should feel safe, comfortable, accepted, and free to express themselves." Vino slipped his fingers through hers behind the podium for support. She didn't look at him, but the squeeze she gave back was all he needed. Her face remained stony. "But ironically, this school has a bully problem."

The principal became worried as a few whispers filtered through the room.

"If the world pushes you down, you take it out on others, right?" Lenne continued. "You feel weak, so you beat on others to feel strong. Can you honestly say that's the right thing to do? Beating someone down, physically or emotionally, without a shred of remorse? Making others feel hopeless, weak, and humiliated, or injuring them enough to send them to the hospital? It's shocking!

Vino and I report these incidents, and yet they continue."

Vino took over. "What's wrong with this school? What the hell have we come to, man? Every single day, people are shoved against lockers, beaten up, mocked for their hair, their clothes."

"And this school's not doing a damn thing about it," Lenne complained. "Things settle for a week or so when we complain, but then it picks up where it left off. This can't go on; it's inhumane! You know what? Shame on you!"

More students began whispering.

"You jerks think you can get away with it," Baldovino said. "You think if you keep the victims down, they won't snitch. Well, then we'll name you because we can't take it anymore. Jennifer Jones, Michael Robinson ...."

Kids began gasping and whispering louder, looking around, some chuckling. The principal rushed over to stop them.

"No," Lenne said, holding up a hand. "If big action isn't taken, this will never be fixed. We've had enough!"

Vino continued. "Lucas Carter, Jesse Ellis, Anna Hall," and the names continued.

"Let's not forget our football team," Lenne said, "and their buddies on the swimming team."

"Everyone knows about you now," Vino said. "If it doesn't get sorted out, if you guys don't get yourselves in check, I'll start an uprising if I have to! Get it together, people. Honestly."

They stepped away from the podium, and by the time everyone left the assembly hall, people everywhere were talking.

Lenne let out a sigh. "That was nerve-racking. You okay?"

Vino grinned. "Never better. We were so badass up there." He leaned in and whispered to her, "Just sayin', with everything you said, the way you were putting them all in their place … that was awesome."

"All right," Dainen breathed out, carefully pressing the place Hugo had indicated under Essai's chin. He felt a button shift inside. He held it in for exactly three seconds before withdrawing his hand and waited. He swallowed nervously. For a moment, he thought he'd screwed up somewhere, but then Essai's eyes half-opened.

Dainen immediately went to cup his face. "Thank goodness," he whispered. "Essai, can you hear me?"

The boy murmured drowsily, "My voice recognition software and speakers are operational."

Dainen sighed in relief. "How many fingers am I holding up?"

"Three fingers."

"Can you sit up?"

Essai blinked, then braced a hand beside him on the couch and slowly pulled himself upright.

"How are you feeling? Does anything feel broken? Uncomfortable? Odd?"

Essai moved his arms and legs to test them, then turned his head from side to side. Dainen waited in angst. Finally, he said, "Everything seems to be intact."

"Oh, thank God," Dainen rejoiced, pulling the boy into his arms. Essai didn't hug him back, but it didn't matter. "I'm so sorry, Essai," he said into his shoulder, his voice cracking. "This is my fault."

He responded, "You are not responsible. The boy in the music room is responsible."

Dainen pulled away and wiped his face. "I'm failing you, Essai. I'm supposed to protect you, but I'm failing you."

Essai slowly tilted his head but didn't reply.

He sniffed softly and muttered, "Fifty-seven added to seventy-seven is two hundred, right?"

Essai shook his head. "The correct answer is one hundred thirty-four."

Dainen smiled and whispered, "I know. Just checking that you're working right."

Essai nodded, then looked down at his lap. His shoulders sagged a little.

"Are you all right?" Dainen asked.

Softly he said, "I am not feeling sick." He looked up again. "Did Hugo feel sick? Is that why he died?"

Dainen froze. This was the first time Essai had ever asked about Hugo. "He … had a heart attack. I don't think he was sick."

"I see. What is it like to feel sick?"

"I don't really know how to explain. Why?"

Essai was quiet for a moment. Then he shook his head and got to his feet. "I seem to be working perfectly. However, I need to recharge."

Dainen watched with confusion as the boy walked out the door.

EIGHT

The sounds of Essai's pan flute were interrupted by a knock on the front door. It had been two days since the incident at school. Dainen had decided to keep him at home for at least a week to recover and think of a plan for where to go next.

He made his way to the door and on the porch stood a boy and a girl, about sixteen years old. He recognised the boy. The girl matched one of Essai's earlier descriptions.

He said, "Baldovino and Lenne, I presume."

"That's right," Baldovino said with a grin. "You must be Dainen. I remember you. Hey, is Essai here? Thought we'd check on him and see how he's doing." He winced. "Unless he's still … broken."

Dainen smiled. "I fixed him. He's in the living room. First, though," he lowered his voice and stepped closer so only they could hear him, "I've been meaning to ask. How did you figure out that Essai is … umm …."

"An artificial human?" Lenne interrupted. "He told us. We didn't believe him at first, of course. I only believed it when I accidentally opened his charging port the other day."

"If you're worried about us spilling the beans," Baldovino said, "our lips are sealed." He made a gesture across his lips to demonstrate.

"I see. Thank you." The fact that they didn't seem too bothered or freaked out was odd, but Dainen didn't ask any further.

"Oh, by the way," Baldovino said, "we stirred up a bit of chaos at school. Gave them all a good scolding, you know?"

"We addressed the school," Lenne said to clarify, "and publicly called out all the bullies. It may be too early to tell, but we haven't seen any more trouble. And most of the ones called out were suspended or expelled. Not sure if it'll last, but it's a start."

Dainen blinked at them. "You guys did that? By yourselves? For Essai?"

"Yeah," Baldovino said proudly, sticking his chest out. "All us. But we didn't say his name, so he's anonymous. And we called out all the bullies we know of, so we didn't just save Essai."

Lenne smirked at his gloating.

"I can't believe this," Dainen breathed. "Thank you. I

don't know what to say. That was incredibly brave. Please, come in."

They wiped their feet before entering, and Dainen called Essai over. As the two of them went to greet him, Dainen made his way to the kitchen, where he'd seen a bowl of sweets somewhere in the cupboard. He dug around until he found it and checked some of the wrapped-up chocolates to see if they were still edible. Then he returned to the living room where the three of them were talking.

"Here," he said, holding out the bowl. "A reward."

Baldovino's mouth fell open.

"Are you sure?" Lenne asked carefully.

"Very sure. I don't eat sweets, and Essai doesn't eat at all. I can't do anything with it. Take it, please."

Lenne grinned as she accepted the sweets. "Thank you, Sir. *Tesoro*, look! It's got some of my favourites!"

"That reminds me," Baldovino said, "we got Essai somethin' too." He dug in his pocket and brought out a keychain, on which hung a tiny green pan flute. He held it out for Essai. "We see you dragging your pan flute everywhere and playing it during break times. Dunno if you have keys, but if you ever get a car one day, you can use this."

Essai took the keychain and examined it. "Interesting," he commented. "I shall save it for when I require it."

"I guess that's his way of saying thank you," Dainen chuckled.

"I've got to say, I never imagined myself hanging with

a robot," Baldovino said. "Sorry for not believing you, man."

"Well, he wasn't exactly supposed to tell anyone," Dainen said, shooting Essai a look.

Essai simply replied, "They will not tell anyone. Since they do not mean harm, there is no harm in them knowing."

Dainen sighed but then smiled. "Don't worry. It worked out in the end."

"Did you make him?" Lenne asked, almost admiringly.

Dainen smiled at the thought. "I'm surprised I even got him working again. No, it was a man named Hugo Grey. He … passed away. I'm taking care of Essai now."

Something flickered in Essai's eyes. Dainen had seen it before. But it disappeared as quickly as it had appeared.

When Dainen returned from work on Friday, he found Essai's pan flute on the couch where he always played, but Essai wasn't there. He always took his flute with him if he went to his room. Maybe he just went to do something and would be back in a minute.

"Essai, I'm home," he called.

It had been a stressful day, so Dainen went for a shower. He returned to the living room, where the pan flute still lay on the couch, without its owner. He called for Essai once more, but no answer came. It was too quiet.

He went upstairs but didn't find him in his room, and then his eyes drifted towards the far end of the hallway. A door was open. The door to the room he'd never been into – Hugo's bedroom. Quietly he approached and peered inside. And there he was, lying on his side, on Hugo's bed, staring at an empty spot on the carpet.

Dainen hesitated before entering. "Essai?" he said softly. "Are you all right?"

A few of Hugo's woollen jackets and scarves lay scattered on the floor, and the closet door was open a crack. He switched on the light, making Essai flinch.

Essai said, barely audible, "I am not feeling sick."

Dainen slowly walked over and sat down on the bed's edge. Essai moved his legs back a bit to make room. "This isn't like you," he said in a hushed voice. "You're usually more … active. Reading, or playing music, or other things."

For a while, Essai didn't reply. Then he said, "I do not feel like it."

Dainen's eyes scanned over all the scattered jackets on the floor. "What are you doing here?" he asked gently.

"Hugo's room is messy, so I decided to clean it. His closet is the most disorganised. But his clothes … smell like him. So does his bed." Essai's voice was neutral, but something was off. He'd said he was all right – he didn't look it.

Dainen didn't know what else to say except, "Do you want company?"

"I want to be alone for now."

Dainen pressed his lips together and, having nothing left to say, got up and left Hugo's room, switching off the light. Essai didn't come out for the rest of the day. Only late that night, when Dainen was in bed, he heard Hugo's door close and soft footsteps make their way to Essai's room. And then the low, faint hum of the charging machine.

The next day, he was entirely normal again. Essai's form of normal, anyway. It was almost worrying.

"Baldovino called me on my cellphone," Essai announced as he entered the kitchen, where Dainen was making himself breakfast. "He suggested that Lenne and I go to his house for a gaming day."

Dainen glanced at him over his shoulder. "Oh? That sounds exciting. If you want to go, of course you can."

Essai hesitated, which he didn't often do. "I … cannot want anything."

Dainen paused with what he was doing as he recalled Essai the previous day, saying, "I want to be alone for now." But he didn't mention it. After a moment's pause, he continued to slice up a tomato. "I think it would be great for you to go."

Essai nodded, "I will," then turned and left the kitchen. Dainen tried not to read too much into him, but he couldn't help it. He seemed mostly like his uncaring, emotionless self, but still, there were those tiny little hints.

While Essai was away at Baldovino's house, Dainen decided that the best thing to do was to get rid of some of Hugo's clothes. He didn't want Essai torturing himself further. He could give it all to charity, and he was sure Hugo wouldn't mind.

By the time Essai returned home, he had already packed things in boxes, ready to put into the car. But on his way out of Hugo's room, Essai blocked his path at the door. Dainen's shoulders jerked, and he released a breath. "You scared me. How was it?"

He wasn't sure how he'd expected the boy to react, but it certainly wasn't for him to take hold of the box and try to yank it out of his grip.

"What are you doing?" Dainen frowned, pulling back. "Let go." Essai pulled again, harder this time, but Dainen held on firmly. "Stop, Essai."

"No," he said, with the slightest hint of curtness in his voice. He yanked with everything he had, and Dainen finally lost his grip. The momentum sent Essai falling hard onto his back, taking the box with him, clothes flying out.

Dainen gasped and instantly went to his rescue, clearing all the clothes that had spilt over him. "You okay?"

Essai sat up, gathered up a few clothes and jumped to his feet, quickly backing away with them in his arms.

Dainen softened. "I see what this is. Look, I get it. But I can't let you torture yourself this way. Just talk to me, I can help you. We will get through this."

Essai dropped the clothes he'd been holding and said nothing as he turned and walked out of the room, a slight sag in his shoulders.

When Dainen returned after dropping off the last boxes at the charity shop, Essai wasn't in the living room. He hung up the keys, then a loud banging noise made him anxious. His eyes went to the stairs. There was another bang, like something was being hit. It came from upstairs. A burglar? Couldn't be, the door had been locked. Had they come through the windows?

Dainen ran upstairs. The noise was coming from Essai's room. Panic surged through him as he rushed to the door. "Essai," he said in alarm as he stormed in. Then he froze. Essai wasn't in danger – he was kicking his desk repeatedly, staring blankly at the floor.

"What are you doing?" Dainen shouted over the noise.

Essai stopped but didn't look at him as he asked, "Where is Hugo?"

Dainen's heart was still out of rhythm. He said though it pained him, "Hugo's gone."

He kicked the desk one more time. "I want Hugo." Another kick, then another. "I want Hugo back."

Dainen caught him by the waist and pulled him back. "Enough, Essai," he whispered.

He pulled himself out of his grip, turned and walked

toward his bed. His steps were less robotic and almost melancholy. He slowly secured himself under the covers, and Dainen was left staring at a curled-up lump on the bed.

"Essai," he tried, but the lump didn't stir. "Please talk to me. It can't go on like this."

Still no reply and no movement. Dainen's throat tightened, and he swallowed. Not knowing what else to do, he turned and left the room, gently closing the door behind him.

"Hugo," he muttered, "what do I do now?"

It was good to finally have Essai back at school, and Lenne believed the gaming day had lifted Essai's spirits — if an artificial human's spirits could be lifted. He'd quickly figured out how to handle the PS4 controller, and Baldovino threw a tantrum every time Essai beat him at Mortal Kombat. Lenne wasn't a big fan of those games, but watching Vino lose so often in the game he was supposed to be a pro at, was rather amusing.

During lunch, Lenne spotted Essai sitting alone at a table in the dining hall. Vino said he had to go hand in a project before joining them.

Essai seemed strange, but she couldn't quite tell why. He was different.

She approached him and took a seat. "Hey. You all right?"

His lips parted slowly, and he whispered, "I might be feeling sick."

She frowned. "How? You can't feel sick."

He seemed to consider her words. "I thought so too. My illness is different. It is like pain, but there is no wound. And I cannot see it."

Lenne said nothing but leaned forward to listen.

"It is not there for me to touch, yet it is still there. I cannot see it, but I know that it exists. I may be sick, but I have no symptoms of any known disease."

She smiled sympathetically. "Is this pain … inside?" She reached over the table to tap a finger against his chest.

Essai didn't answer for a moment. Then he said, "I do not know."

"I think what you're explaining is a feeling."

He shook his head. "I cannot feel," he stated.

"Are you sure about that?" she said slowly. "Maybe it's not as impossible as you think. You're AI. You can think for yourself. Maybe you can feel for yourself too."

For the first time, Essai seemed unsure.

"Well, what's causing this experience?" Lenne asked.

"Hugo," he said plainly.

"Your creator? The one who passed away?"

Essai didn't seem to know how to respond to the question.

"Oh," she said softly, "I know what this is. You miss him."

"What's up, losers?" Vino burst in and plopped down next to Lenne. "The rock star is back in the—" He stopped and read the room. His smile faded. "What happened?"

Lenne filled him in, and his shoulders sagged. "Oh," he said, "sorry to hear that, dude. I want to say I know how you feel…" his voice turned softer, "it's just you might not feel it the same way that I do. But I lost someone too."

Lenne diverted her eyes and swallowed. It had been a long time since Vino had talked about this story.

"My big sister," he continued. "She was nineteen when I lost her in a car accident three years ago. I was about thirteen. She was driving me home from school when some idiot skipped a red light, and it ended bad – real bad. She was taken to a hospital, but … she didn't make it."

Essai looked at him a while longer. When it was clear Vino's story was finished, he turned his eyes back to the table. "My condolences."

Vino smiled softly. "Thanks. What I'm saying is, I know what it's like to lose someone you love."

Essai blinked. "Love?"

"Yeah, I loved my sister. We were close. I don't think about it as much as I used to, but I still miss her. Sometimes I can't help it."

Essai's face made a funny expression like he was trying to decide whether or not to do something. Finally, he slowly reached over the table. His hand wavered before very awkwardly tapping Vino's shoulder. He said in a one-tone voice, "There, there."

Despite it all, both Baldovino and Lenne burst out laughing.

"Not very good with this kind of stuff, are you?" Vino chuckled. "That's all right. Neither am I, to be honest. Look, I know you feel like garbage right now, like everything's just hell and the world's out to get you. But in time, all wounds heal. Even those inside, at least a little."

Essai was quiet again.

"You know, I've known Lenne a long time. We knew each other when my sister died, and she helped me get through it. Honestly, I don't know if I'd be whole right now if not for her." His hand went to hers, and she smiled as their fingers entwined. "So, sometimes you need people in your life to help you heal. We'll be here for you."

"Here … for me?"

"Yeah, we've got your back. You know, if you need someone to talk to or shoulders to cry on. Or even just to play a video game with or whatever – we got you." He extended a fist.

Essai went to open it so he could shake.

Baldovino stopped his hand, formed it into a fist and punched it with his own. He grinned and said, "You'll get it eventually."

NINE

Essai hadn't said a word all day, no matter what he tried. Dainen was entirely lost. How was he supposed to comfort a robot? He didn't know what Essai was feeling exactly, and he wasn't sure Essai did either. Dainen paced around in his room, trying to come up with a plan. Nothing came to mind, so he decided just to wing it.

When he returned downstairs, the music had stopped. The pan flute lay in Essai's open hands on his lap as he quietly stared ahead of him.

Dainen carefully approached. "Are you okay?"

He got to his feet but didn't go anywhere. Silence hung over the room for a long while, and it quickly became uncomfortable.

Finally, Essai broke the silence with a soft, "I do not know." He didn't meet Dainen's eyes. "I do not have an answer. I always have answers."

Dainen stood in front of him. "Sometimes, to handle our emotions, we must express them or let them out. It's all right to cry if you need to."

Essai shook his head. "I am a machine. I am unable to cry."

Dainen swallowed and lowered his eyes. "Oh," was all he replied.

"I cannot feel," Essai continued. "But Lenne says it is a feeling and that it is inside. But inside of me is a machine. What does a feeling look like? If I cannot see it, it is not real. If it is not real, how am I feeling it? How can humans feel it?" His shoulders sank, and he whispered, "What is happening to me?"

Dainen let out a sympathetic sigh and gently took hold of his arms. "It's nothing to be afraid of. Maybe you shouldn't question it. Instead, just let it happen."

Essai stood still a moment. Then he weaved forward and collapsed into him, taking Dainen by surprise. His thin arms wrapped around his waist in a firm hold, not enough to hurt but enough to assure Dainen couldn't move.

"Hugo always did this to me," Essai whispered. "He called it a hug. You did it to me once too. I apologise for not returning it."

Dainen didn't need to hear more. He wrapped one arm around the boy's shoulders and used his free hand to lightly stroke his hair. Essai only pulled away several minutes later and then returned to his couch to continue playing his flute.

Dainen watched the boy with some sadness, and then he had an idea. He went out to the shops and returned to find Essai reading at his desk.

Dainen stepped in with a smile. "I have something for you." He held it up for him to see.

"A book," Essai observed.

"It's a diary." He placed it on his desk. "I think it might help you a great deal."

Essai tilted his head. "I do not know how to write in a diary. What will I require it for?"

"You've been going through a lot lately. It may be easier for you to express your feelings if you write them down. If you don't know how you feel, write about that too. That's the nice thing about diaries. Only you will read it, so you can write whatever you want."

Essai considered it. "I will try."

<hr>

The day was dragging on forever. Vino hated Mondays. By the time the bell rang for lunch, it felt like it was supposed to be time to go home. Baldovino really couldn't wait for school to be over.

He searched around the dining hall until he found where Essai was sitting. When he arrived, the first thing Essai said was, "How do you use a diary?"

Vino raised an eyebrow as he sat. "Hey yourself."

"Dainen gave me a diary, but I don't know how to write in it."

Vino frowned a little in thought. "Well, umm, I guess you just write stuff down about your life."

"How do I do that?"

"I don't know, I'm not a good writer. Hey, tell you what. Lenne writes in diaries all the time. She has hundreds of them. She's kind of an expert. Maybe ask her."

Essai looked up at the ceiling, his expression remaining blank. But something flickered in his eyes. Vino gave him a lopsided smile. "You'll get there, dude."

When Lenne arrived, Essai asked her the same question.

"Oh, it's easy," she said. "You write the date and start with, 'Today this and that happened to me, and here's how I feel about it'."

Essai blinked at her. "I will need elaboration."

"Okay. For example, 'Today I found out that my cousin is coming over this weekend, and I'm dreading it. I don't like my cousin. She's annoying and never baths'."

Essai tilted his head. "But I do not have a cousin."

"That was just an example. The main issue is you miss Hugo, right? So write about it."

"I do not know if I miss him or what I am feeling. Or I do, but I do not know how to put it into words."

"That's okay. You can draw it if you want."

"I am not a visual artist."

"Don't think about it too much," Lenne said with a shrug. "It'll come to you."

Essai stared at the diary's blank pages for hours. No ink touched the paper. It was hard for Dainen to watch. In some way, it seemed to be annoying Essai. Day by day, he just sat and stared at it. The more Dainen tried to help, the more frustrated Essai became with his failed efforts. Dainen wished he could give him the simple straight answers he needed, but he'd never written in a diary himself. He hadn't expected it to be so difficult for Essai.

"Okay, write down how you feel. Start with the basics," Dainen said.

"What basics? My name and residence?"

"Maybe try something a little deeper. Like saying you recently lost Hugo."

"That is not a feeling. It is a fact." His voice was almost snappy. Or was it Dainen's imagination?

"Of course, but it's an event. After that, try saying how you feel about it."

"I don't know!" Essai screamed.

Dainen was taken aback.

"I am tired of you asking me that! I know how I should feel – I should feel sad that Hugo's gone, I should feel upset, and I should miss him, but I do not know how that is supposed to feel. I liked doing things with Hugo. I liked going on walks with him, reading with him, playing music for him, and playing chess with him. But then he went away one day and did not even say goodbye!"

Dainen was too stunned to say anything.

"And then you showed up. You said Hugo asked you to protect me, and you act like you know what you are doing, but you don't! You are not Hugo, and you can never replace him. Only Hugo can be Hugo. I want him back. He told me he cared about me, so why did he leave? Why did he leave without saying goodbye? He left me alone with you, and I don't even know you well. But I cannot simply adapt. You are not Hugo!"

Dainen didn't try to calm him down. He let him shout. He took every lash of words that came his way. Because this was what Essai needed – he needed to let go.

Finally, Essai let out something like a whimper and fell to his knees. He said nothing further and stared with wide eyes at the carpet, surprised at his own display.

Dainen waited a few minutes before crouching before him. "You did it," he whispered. "That's it, right there. You did it, Essai. See? Sometimes you just need to let it out. I'm proud of you."

Essai stared at him. And finally – finally – Dainen saw emotion on the boy's face. Anger. Sadness. Grief. Pain. All of it.

"Are you not upset?" Essai asked softly, his voice cracking unexpectedly. "I've said hurtful things. You should be sad. Or angry."

"I'm not." He cupped Essai's face with one hand. "I was never trying to replace Hugo. No person is replaceable. I know he meant a lot to you and that you loved him."

Essai shivered just slightly. "Love?"

"Yes. And Hugo loved you very much. You weren't like a son to him. You *were* his son." Dainen whispered, "I know he left without saying goodbye, but it was out of his control. He never meant to hurt you. You're right, we may not know each other as well as we should, so maybe we should get to know each other better. I promised him I'd take care of you. Will you let me?"

After a long silence, Essai finally nodded slowly. "All right," he whispered.

Dainen looked at him more seriously. "Tell me, Essai, do you want to be human?"

He seemed confused. "What do you mean?"

Hugo had written in his journals that he'd created a chip that would allow Essai to age as a human, but he had never installed it. Not because it was a complex procedure but because he hadn't wanted Essai to age. He'd only designed it in case Essai came to need it – or want it.

Hugo wrote that Essai's default age was set to sixteen. This chip would react with all the mechanisms, the synthetic cells in his body, and his artificial skin. He would not grow, as his mechanical bone structure couldn't stretch or expand, but his skin would age, eventually getting wrinkles, and his hair would turn grey. And when the right time came, Essai would shut down. So, the chip and everything with it functioned as a timer.

He had carried this knowledge for a while but wasn't sure if he'd wanted to use it. But given how things were progressing with Essai, Dainen felt it was time to share it. At the end of the day, it was Essai's decision, not his own.

He discussed this with him and explained everything that came with ageing, all the pros and cons, virtues and struggles.

Finally, after taking it all in, Essai said, "Yes. It was fascinating to watch Hugo live. To see him eat, drink, sleep without recharging his energy the way I do. It seemed to take up much of his time, but I sometimes wondered what it would be like for me to live that way."

"Think about this carefully," Dainen said. "Making you age and then removing it all later could have severe side effects on your body. Hugo said you could malfunction. If you decide to do this, there's no going back."

Essai only thought a few more minutes. Then he said again, "Yes. I want to live like Hugo did."

TEN

It was Wednesday. Dainen had a day off, and due to some sporting event at school, Essai got to stay home, which meant they had the whole day together.

When Dainen dragged himself downstairs in his pyjamas to make himself a coffee, Essai was sitting cross-legged on the carpet. His pan flute hung around his neck, and a book lay open before him. The diary, Dainen realised. He'd drawn horizontal lines between the existing ones.

Dainen raised his brow in interest as he neared. "What are you doing?"

Essai played a short, five-note tune before saying, "I do not know. I will see when I am finished."

"Right. Okay." Dainen went to the kitchen. He heard another short tune, a long pause, and another tune. He got his cup ready, and while the kettle boiled, he checked

Essai's progress. A few musical notes were drawn on the lines of the page.

"You're writing a song," Dainen breathed in wonder.

"Yes." He played another few tunes and scribbled random notes on a separate page. Next, he played a longer melody. When he finished, he looked at the ceiling for a moment, then drew a few more notes.

For the next few weeks, every day after homework, Essai continued writing his song. For hours, all Dainen heard were little music snippets and scribbling on paper. Essai's face was emotionless, but now and then, something appeared in his eyes, something hard to make out. And Dainen would just stand there, watching quietly and curiously as the boy worked. At times, Essai drew a thick line across a page, crossing the whole thing out and starting over. He certainly had no problem filling the diary pages anymore.

Then finally, one Friday night, Essai knocked on the door of Dainen's room.

"What is it, Essai?" Dainen yawned.

"I want to say something to Hugo," he replied. "Please take me to him."

Dainen remained quiet as he tried to make sense of his request. "You want to see Hugo?" It took Dainen a while, but at last, he understood. "Oh, I see. All right, then, when do you want to go?"

"Now."

"Right now? It's 10 p.m."

"Yes," Essai stated.

Well, if not now, it may never happen, Dainen thought. "I'll get my coat."

He pulled the car to a stop outside the cemetery gate. The only sounds came from crickets, an owl, and a faint breeze. Otherwise, it was quiet. He got out, shuddered at the cold, and followed Essai through the gate into the graveyard. They walked down a narrow stone path until Essai stopped at the tombstone on which Hugo's name was engraved. He stared at the name without saying a word.

"Umm," Dainen said quietly, "do you want me to leave you two alone for a bit?"

Essai just nodded, his eyes fixed on the grave. So Dainen turned and walked, stopping by a tree a little farther away. He leaned against it. It was cold, but he didn't care. He'd wait there for as long as Essai needed him to.

Essai had to work hard at processing all the thoughts flowing through him. He sat down, crossed his legs, reached into his jacket pocket, and pulled out his pan flute.

The one Hugo had given to him. He stared at it for a while, processing more rushing thoughts.

Finally, he brought the instrument to his lips, closed his eyes, and began playing the familiar tune he had taken so long to complete. His thoughts quietened, and he was calm. Music flowed from him freely, along with the long hissing grass, the leaves of trees, and the crickets in the distance. He focused on every note, making sure they could all be heard, assuring they all rose and fell exactly the way they had to so that Hugo would understand what they meant – so Hugo would know how much he meant to him.

Dainen watched in awe as the beautiful song filled the air.

"There are a lot of people here," Essai noted.

Baldovino shrugged. "Well, it is the weekend."

"Why did you bring us to a cinema?" Essai asked. "You can watch a movie at home."

"We thought you might enjoy it since you've never been to a cinema," Lenne smiled. "It is a nuisance when you need to go to the bathroom, though, because they don't pause the movie for you."

"I don't have a bladder," Essai said.

"Lucky," Lenne grumbled.

They sat down in three empty seats in the third row. Baldovino held out the popcorn. "Want some?"

"I don't eat."

"Oh, yeah, forgot. Damn, what a shame. L, you want some?"

She had her own, yet she took a few from his bucket. The movie started, and beside him, Baldovino grinned, resting his arm on the backrest behind Lenne's head and stuffing a handful of popcorn into his mouth.

Essai watched the people move on the screen. He

didn't know why, but he found himself leaning forward. He frequently whispered questions to Baldovino, who seemed glad to answer. He'd never been this intrigued by a movie.

There was a scene where a policeman pointed a gun at a criminal lying on the ground and said, "You've got to ask yourself one question: 'Do I feel lucky?' Well, do ya, punk?"

Everyone in the cinema laughed, and Baldovino seemed to find it especially humorous. Essai did not understand the appeal. He only found the scene interesting when the man pulled the trigger, but no bullet fired. Baldovino and Lenne laughed again.

Essai murmured, "Why would he threaten a man with a gun if there is no ammunition inside?"

Baldovino shrugged and whispered, "Dunno, just to scare him, I guess. And to make it funny."

Essai narrowed his eyes. The man with the gun seemed to find it funny as well, for he laughed as he walked away. It was bizarre, but somehow Essai understood. He didn't see the point of all the bloodshed, but the entire scene was ironic, considering the utter fear of the criminal when faced with the empty gun.

Suddenly, there were odd leaps in Essai's stomach. Was there something wrong with the wiring inside him? He had to have that checked later, but it didn't feel like something was wrong. And then he felt his mouth do something peculiar – the corners pulled up, all on their own, out of his control. It was utterly abnormal, but strangely, he liked it.

When the movie ended, the three of them chatted as they walked through the parking lot toward Baldovino's parents, who had come to pick them up.

"How did you like the movie?" Lenne asked, nudging Essai on the arm.

"It was intriguing."

Baldovino grinned. "Had fun, did you?"

"I believe so. The movie did not make much sense, and there seemed to be no benefit to all the fighting. However, analysing the scenes was fascinating. I believe it would be appropriate to join such an event again."

Baldovino laughed. "Listen to you! 'Appropriate.' Well, good for you, dude!" He threw an arm around Essai's shoulders.

"*Ciao* Vino," his father greeted as they bundled into the car.

"You enjoy?" His mother's broken English had a strong Italian accent.

"*Sì, Mamma,*" said Vino excitedly. "Yes, we enjoyed it very much."

Something baffled Essai during the car ride. Baldovino said to his mother, "Love you, *Mamma.*"

He'd heard that word before. Love. Essai wondered if he was actually able to feel love. When he thought of the word, his mind went to two people – Hugo and Dainen.

"Hey, Essai," Baldovino said. "You free next weekend?"

"Free?"

"I mean, do you have plans? Or can we hang out?"

"Yes. I am, as you put it, free."

Lenne chuckled.

"I thought we could play a game. We could all jam together. Sound good?"

Essai lifted his chin. "Mr and Mrs Morelli, do you approve of me coming over to play video games with Vino?"

"*Certo*, Essai. Yes, of course," his mother said.

He felt a nudge on his shoulder and turned his head to see Baldovino looking at him with amazement and the biggest grin ever. "Dude! You called me Vino!"

Essai blinked. "I do not recall that."

"Just now. You called me Vino! Lenne, you heard that, right?"

Essai focused ahead of him. "In which case, I meant to say Baldovino."

He laughed. "Wow! You called me Vino. Know what that means? It means we're officially best friends." He held out a fist. Essai hesitated.

"Come on, man," Vino moaned, "I thought you'd have it by now."

Slowly Essai put out a fist and bumped Vino's, who was beside himself with excitement.

"What about me?" Lenne whined. She held out her fist too, and Essai did the same. Satisfied, she shifted in her seat and smiled.

Dainen watched the red car pull into the driveway. The door opened, and Essai emerged, then Baldovino and Lenne. They spoke for a minute while Vino's parents waved at Dainen. He smiled, waving back. He was pleasantly surprised when he witnessed Essai and his friend fist bump. Essai watched the car drive away, then walked up the path leading to the house.

"Hey, Essai," he said. "How was it?"

Essai seemed apprehensive as he took a few steps. Suddenly, he ran towards Dainen, crashed into him and wrapped his arms tightly around his waist. Dainen took a step back. "Woah," he gasped. "Did you miss me?"

With his head buried in Dainen's chest, Essai spoke. And the words made Dainen freeze.

"I love you."

A moment of silence hung in the air. Then a smile slowly crept onto Dainen's face. He folded his hand over the back of the boy's blonde head and said, "I love you too, Essai."

They broke apart, and Essai looked up at him. His mouth twitched, and as if Dainen hadn't had enough surprises already – he smiled. A bit awkwardly, but still.

That was it. That smile confirmed for Dainen that he was no longer only doing this for Hugo. Not even for himself. It was all about Essai.

"I'm sorry I insulted you a few weeks ago and shouted at you," Essai said. "You offered me much assistance, and

I believe I would be worse off without it. You are not Hugo, but you are Dainen, and I am grateful to you."

"You don't have to thank me, Essai," he smiled warmly. "I'd do it again, as many times as I needed to, and it would be my absolute pleasure. Come. Let's go inside."

Essai nodded.

It was quiet in the graveyard, even in the afternoon. The only sound was the occasional birdsong. It was mostly empty, and the only other person there had left a few minutes ago.

Dainen approached the familiar tombstone and smiled as he crouched down to place the flowers he'd gathered from a nearby field. He remained in that position for a long time, staring at the stone, wondering where to start.

Finally, he said, "Hey, Hugo. Wherever you are – if you're anywhere – I hope you're doing well. Essai spoke to you the other night through his song. I hope you heard it. He spent countless hours preparing it for you. It's an original song, and I'm sure you'd be very proud of him."

Dainen paused and grinned at the absurdity of speaking to Hugo's tombstone but realised that if Essai found peace, he might too.

"I guess I also have a few things to say," he smiled.

"Do keep in mind, I don't have a music piece to play you. I'm not that creative."

He paused and took a deep breath before continuing. "Essai misses you − a lot. He's still trying to figure that out, but I want you to know he's doing well. He's going to school. I thought it would be a good idea to give him some human experience, you know? There have been some obstacles, and they probably won't be the last, but he'll get through them. I'll help him with that. He's made good friends too. I know it's hard to tell with him some-times, but … I think he's happy, even if he can't describe it yet."

The birds chirped as if to remind him of something.

"Oh, that ageing chip you wrote about? Yeah, I read your journal. Sorry, I couldn't help myself. I installed it, and I'll have you know, it wasn't easy. Nearly shocked myself. You could've done a background check on my IT skills before choosing me, you know." Dainen chuckled. "But, I managed, somehow, and now Essai will age. I'm not sure what you would think of that, but it's what he wants. So I thought you'd be all right with it. Well, I hope so. Otherwise, I screwed up."

Silence filled the air as Dainen gathered his thoughts.

"Hugo, I don't know why you picked me to care for Essai. Maybe you felt I was the only one available, or perhaps you liked the look of me. Hell, maybe it was just coincidence. But whatever the case, I'm glad you did. I've grown rather, well, attached to Essai. I've never had children, and sure, he's not like most children, but I've come to love him."

Dainen felt a surge of emotion and had to hold back a few tears.

"It is an absolute honour and joy to care for Essai. I will continue to put in the work, time and commitment because it's worth it. Because he deserves it. Your son will thrive in life, and he's going to be great one day – I just know it."

He took a deep breath, then said, "You've helped me a great deal in this journey, Hugo, even though you may not know it. I've realised I was missing purpose in my life, and I was missing love. And you and Essai have given me both, and I thank you."

Dainen checked his watch and smiled. The birds whistled as he rose from Hugo's grave and hastily left the cemetery. He didn't want to be late collecting Essai from school.

ABOUT THE AUTHOR

Paula van Kerken has always had a passion for writing stories, and at twelve years old, she decided she would be an author and has been writing ever since. The fantasy and supernatural genres bring her the most delight.

Her mother tongue is Afrikaans, but she is fluent in English. She wrote *"The Son of Hugo Grey"* at the young age of seventeen.

Outside of writing, Paula has a strong interest in visual arts and loves to portray the stories in her head through illustrations and paintings.

Paula lives in Johannesburg, South Africa, currently with her parents and her two cats. Paula adores felines and has lived with cats since birth.